First Edition 2019

ISBN 978-0-9990249-3-5
Library of Congress Control Number 2017960164

10 9 8 7 6 5 4 3 2 1
Printed in China

The art work for this book was hand-drawn in ink and edited digitally.
This book was typeset in Futura PT Heavy.

Ripple Grove
Press 🗝
Shelburne, Vermont
RippleGrovePress.com

Thank you for reading.

For my sister, Emily.

The
Full House
and the
Empty House

LK James

Ripple Grove
Press

There once were two houses
who lived on a hill.

On the outside
they looked much the same.

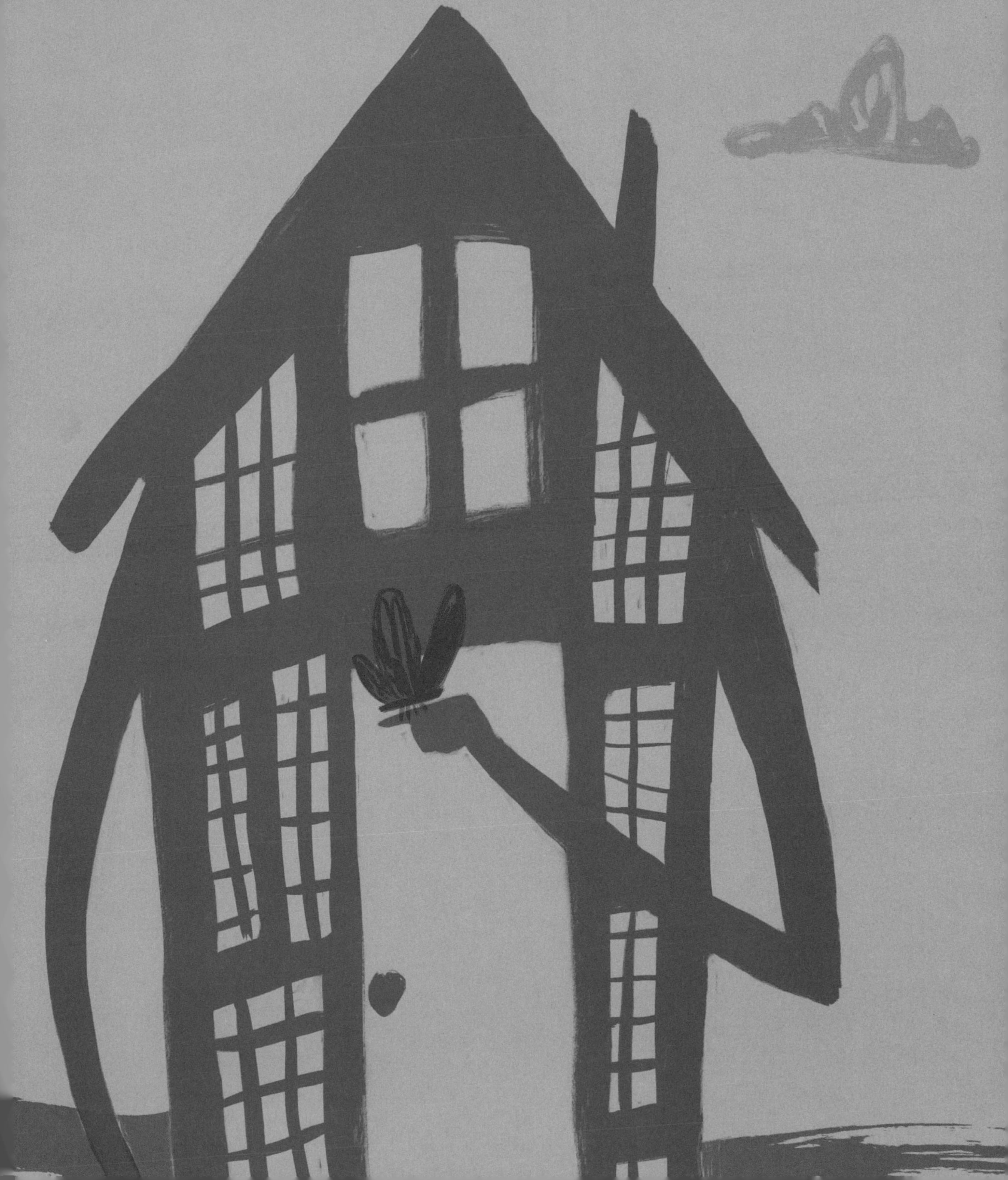

But on the inside—

—the two houses were quite different.

The kitchen of the full house
was full of many kitchen-y things.

The shelves were stacked
with plates, cups, and bowls.

The cupboards were stuffed
with boxes of crackers,
cans of sardines,
and jars of fancy jellies.

In the kitchen of the empty house

was just a sandwich on a plate.

The bathroom of the full house
was full of many bathroom-y things.

There was a big bathtub with gold clawed feet,
a sink shaped like a seashell,
a hairbrush and comb made of bone,
and cakes of lilac soap.

In the bathroom of the empty house
was just a toilet and a sink.

Despite their differences within,
the two houses were close friends.

When they danced,
all the things inside the full house
made an enormous noise—

—as they crashed and flew about.

It sounded like a symphony
to the empty house,
and made the empty house feel
like it too was full of many things.

And because the empty house was empty,

the full house could swing the empty house
into the air with ease.

And when the empty house
was high above the ground,
the full house felt like it too was flying.

In the evening when the two houses
grew tired of dancing,

they would rest on the hillside
and look out at the world together—

—until it was time to go home.